Xenophon

The Polity of the Athenians and the Lacedaemonians

Outlook

Xenophon

The Polity of the Athenians and the Lacedaemonians

1. Auflage | ISBN: 978-3-73262-091-3

Erscheinungsort: Frankfurt am Main, Deutschland

Erscheinungsjahr: 2018

Outlook Verlag GmbH, Frankfurt.

Xenophon

The Polity of the Athenians and the Lacedaemonians

Outlook

THE POLITY OF THE ATHENIANS AND THE LACEDAEMONIANS

By Xenophon

Translation by H. G. Dakyns

Contents

THE POLITY OF THE ATHENIANS

THE POLITY OF THE LACEDAEMONIANS

THE POLITY OF THE ATHENIANS

I

Now, as concerning the Polity of the Athenians, (1) and the type or manner of constitution which they have chosen, (2) I praise it not, in so far as the very choice involves the welfare of the baser folk as opposed to that of the better class. I repeat, I withhold my praise so far; but, given the fact that this is the type agreed upon, I propose to show that they set about its preservation in the right way; and that those other transactions in connection with it, which are looked upon as blunders by the rest of the Hellenic world, are the reverse.

(1) See Grote, "H. G." vi. p. 47 foll.; Thuc. i. 76, 77; viii. 48; Boeckh, "P. E. A." passim; Hartman, "An. Xen. N." cap. viii.; Roquette, "Xen. Vit." S. 26; Newman, "Pol. Arist." i. 538; and "Xenophontis qui fertur libellus de Republica Atheniensium," ed. A. Kirchhoff (MDCCCLXXIV), whose text I have chiefly followed.

(2) Lit. "I do not praise their choice of the (particular) type, in so far as..."

In the first place, I maintain, it is only just that the poorer classes (3) and the People of Athens should be better off than the men of birth and wealth, seeing that it is the people who man the fleet, (4) and put round the city her girdle of power. The steersman, (5) the boatswain, the lieutenant, (6) the look- out-man at the prow, the shipright—these are the people who engird the city with power far rather than her heavy infantry (7) and men of birth of quality. This being the case, it seems only just that offices of state should be thrown open to every one both in the ballot (8) and the show of hands, and that the right of speech should belong to any one who likes, without restriction. For, observe, (9) there are many of these offices which, according as they are in good or in bad hands, are a source of safety or of danger to the People, and in these the People prudently abstains from sharing; as, for instance, it does not think it incumbent on itself to share in the functions of the general or of the commander of cavalry. (10) The sovereign People recognises the fact that in forgoing the personal exercise of these offices, and leaving them to the control of the more powerful (11) citizens, it secures the balance of advantage to itself. It is only those departments of government which bring emolument
(12) and assist the private estate that the People cares to keep in its own hands.

(3) Cf. "Mem." I. ii. 58 foll.

(4) Lit. "ply the oar and propel the galleys."

(5) See "Econ." viii. 14; Pollux, i. 96; Arist. "Knights," 543 foll.; Plat. "Laws," v. 707 A; Jowett, "Plat." v. 278 foll.; Boeckh, "P. E. A." bk. ii. ch. xxi.

(6) Lit. "pentecontarch;" see Dem. "In Pol." 1212.

(7) Aristot. "Pol." vi. 7; Jowett, "The Politics of Aristotle," vol. i. p. 109.

(8) {klerotoi}, {airetoi}.

(9) Reading with Kirchhoff, {epeo tou}, or if {epeita}, "in the next place."

(10) Hipparch.

(11) Cf. "Hipparch." i. 9; "Econ." ii. 8.

(12) E.g. the {dikasteria}.

In the next place, in regard to what some people are puzzled to explain—the fact that everywhere greater consideration is shown to the base, to poor people and to common folk, than to persons of good quality—so far from being a matter of surprise, this, as can be shown, is the keystone of the preservation of the democracy. It is these poor people, this common folk, this riff-raff, (13) whose prosperity, combined with the growth of their numbers, enhances the democracy. Whereas, a shifting of fortune to the advantage of the wealthy and the better classes implies the establishment on the part of the commonalty of a strong power in opposition to itself. In fact, all the world over, the cream of society is in opposition to the democracy. Naturally, since the smallest amount of intemperance and injustice, together with the highest scrupulousness in the pursuit of excellence, is to be found in the ranks of the better class, while within the ranks of the People will be found the greatest amount of ignorance, disorderliness, rascality—poverty acting as a stronger incentive to base conduct, not to speak of lack of education and ignorance, traceable to the lack of means which afflicts the average of mankind. (14)

(13) Or, "these inferiors," "these good-for-nothings."

(14) Or, "some of these folk." The passage is corrupt.

The objection may be raised that it was a mistake to allow the universal right of speech (15) and a seat in council. These should have been reserved for the cleverest, the flower of the community. But here, again, it will be found that they are acting with wise deliberation in granting to (16) even the baser sort the right of speech, for supposing only the better people might speak, or sit in council, blessings would fall to the lot of those like themselves, but to the commonalty the reverse of blessings. Whereas now, any one who likes, any base fellow, may get up and discover something to the advantage of himself and his equals. It may be retorted: "And what sort of advantage either for himself or for the People can such a fellow be expected to hit upon?" The answer to which is, that in their judgment the ignorance and baseness of this fellow, together with his goodwill, are worth a great deal more to them than your superior person's virtue and wisdom, coupled with animosity. What it comes to, therefore, is that a state founded upon such institutions will not be the best state; (17) but, given a democracy, these are the right means to procure its preservation. The People, it must be borne in mind, does not demand that the city should be well governed and itself a slave. It desires to be free and to be master. (18) As to bad legislation it does not concern itself about that. (19) In fact, what you believe to be bad legislation is the very source of the People's strength and freedom. But if you seek for good legislation, in the first place you will see the cleverest members of the community laying down the laws for the rest. And in the next place, the better class will curb and chastise the lower orders; the better class will deliberate in behalf of the state, and not suffer crack-brained fellows to sit in council, or to speak or vote in Parliament. (20) No doubt; but under the weight of such blessings the People will in a very short time be reduced to slavery.

(15) Lit. "everybody to speak in turn."

(16) Or, "it is a counsel of perfection on their part to grant to," etc.

(17) Or, "the ideal state."

(18) Or, "and to govern and hold office."

(19) Or, "it will take the risk of that."

(20) See Grote, "H. G." v. p. 510 note.

Another point is the extraordinary amount of license (21) granted to slaves and resident aliens at Athens, where a blow is illegal, and a slave will not step aside to let you pass him in the street. I will explain the reason of this peculiar custom. Supposing it were legal for a slave to be beaten by a free citizen, or for a resident alien or freedman to be beaten by a citizen, it would frequently happen that an Athenian might be mistaken for a slave or an alien and receive a beating; since the Athenian People is no better clothed than the slave or alien, nor in personal appearance is there any superiority. Or if the fact itself that slaves in Athens are allowed to indulge in luxury, and indeed in some cases to live magnificently, be found astonishing, this too, it can be shown, is done of set purpose. Where you have a naval power (22) dependent upon wealth (23) we must perforce be slaves to our slaves, in order that we may get in our slave-rents, (24) and let the real slave go free. Where you have wealthy slaves it ceases to be advantageous that my slave should stand in awe of you. In Lacedaemon my slave stands in awe of you. (25) But if your slave is in awe of me there will be a risk of his giving away his own moneys to avoid running a risk in his own person. It is for this reason then that we have established an equality between our slaves and free men; and again between our resident aliens and full citizens, (26) because the city stands in need of her resident aliens to meet the requirements of such a multiplicity of arts and for the purposes of her navy. That is, I repeat, the justification for the equality conferred upon our resident aliens.

(21) See Aristot. "Pol." v. 11 and vi. 4; Jowett, op. cit. vol. i. pp. 179, 196; Welldon, "The Politics of Aristotle," pp. 394 323; Dem. "Phil." III. iii. 10; Plaut. "Stich." III. i. 37.

(22) See Diod. xi. 43.

(23) Reading, {apo khrematon, anagke}, or (reading, {apo khrematon anagke}) "considerations of money force us to be slaves."

(24) See Boeckh, "P. E. A." I. xiii. (Eng. trans. p. 72). "The rights of property with regard to slaves in no way differed from any other chattel; they could be given or taken as pledges. They laboured either on their master's account or their own, in consideration of a certain sum to be paid to the master, or they were let out on hire either for the mines or any other kind of labour, and even for other persons' workshops, or as hired servants for wages ({apophora}): a similar payment was also exacted by the masters for their slaves serving in the fleet." Ib. "Dissertation on the Silver Mines of Laurion," p. 659 (Eng. trans.)

(25) See "Pol. Lac." vi. 3.

(26) Or, "we have given to our slaves the right to talk like equals with free men, just as to resident aliens the right of so talking with citizens." See Jebb, "Theophr. Char." xiv. 4, note, p. 221. See Demosth. "against Midias," 529, where the law is cited. "If any one commit a personal outrage upon man, woman, or child, whether free-born or slave, or commit any illegal act against any such person, let any Athenian that chooses" (not being under disability) "indict him before the judges," etc; and the orator exclaims: "You know, O Athenians, the humanity of the law, which allows not even slaves to be insulted in their persons."—C. R. Kennedy.

Citizens devoting their time to gymnastics and to the cultivation of music are not to be found in Athens; (27) the sovereign People has disestablished them, (28) not from any disbelief in the beauty and honour of such training, but recognising the fact that these are things the cultivation of which is beyond its power. On the same principle, in the case of the coregia, (29) the gymnasiarchy, and the trierarchy, the fact is recognised that it is the rich man who trains the chorus, and the People for whom the chorus is trained; it is the rich man who is trierarch or gymnasiarch, and the People that profits by their labours. (30) In fact, what the People looks upon as its right is to pocket the money. (31) To sing and run and dance and man the vessels is well enough, but only in order that the People may be the gainer, while the rich are made poorer. And so in the courts of justice, (32) justice is not more an object of concern to the jurymen than what touches personal advantage.

(27) For {mousike} and {gumnastike}, see Becker's "Charicles," Exc. "Education."

(28) See "Revenues," iv. 52; Arist. "Frogs," 1069, {e xekenosen tas te palaistras}, "and the places of exercise vacant and bare."—Frere.

(29) "The duties of the choregia consisted in finding maintenance and instruction for the chorus" (in tragedy, usually of fifteen

persons) "as long as they were in training; and in providing the dresses and equipments for the performance."—Jebb, "Theophr. Char." xxv. 3. For those of the gymnasiarchy, see "Dict. of Antiq." "Gymnasium." For that of the trierarchy, see Jebb, op. cit. xxv. 9; xxix. 16; Boeckh, "P. E. A." IV. xi.

(30) See "Econ." ii. 6; Thuc. vi. 31.

(31) See Boeckh, "P. E. A." II. xvi. p. 241.

(32) For the system of judicature, the {dikasteria}, and the boards of jurymen or judges, see Aristot. "Constitution of Athens," ch. lxiii.; "Dict. of Antiq." s.v.

To speak next of the allies, and in reference to the point that emissaries (33) from Athens come out, and, according to common opinion, calumniate and vent their hatred (34) upon the better sort of people, this is done (35) on the principle that the ruler cannot help being hated by those whom he rules; but that if wealth and respectability are to wield power in the subject cities the empire of the Athenian People has but a short lease of existence. This explains why the better people are punished with infamy, (36) robbed of their money, driven from their homes, and put to death, while the baser sort are promoted to honour. On the other hand, the better Athenians throw their aegis over the better class in the allied cities. (37) And why? Because they recognise that it is to the interest of their own class at all times to protect the best element in the cities. It may be urged (38) that if it comes to strength and power the real strength of Athens lies in the capacity of her allies to contribute their money quota. But to the democratic mind (39) it appears a higher advantage still for the individual Athenian to get hold of the wealth of the allies, leaving them only enough to live upon and to cultivate their estates, but powerless to harbour treacherous designs.

(33) For {oi ekpleontes}, see Grote, "H. G." vi. p. 41.

(34) Reading {misousi}; or, if with Kirchhoff, {meiousi}, "in every way humiliate."

(35) Or, "(they do so) as recognising the fact."

(36) {atimia} = the loss of civil rights, either total or partial. See C. R. Kennedy, "Select Speeches of Demosthenes," Note 13, Disenfranchisement.

(37) See Thuc. viii. 48.

(38) See Grote, "H. G." vi. 53.

(39) Or, "to a thorough democrat."

Again, (40) it is looked upon as a mistaken policy on the part of the Athenian democracy to compel her allies to voyage to Athens in order to have their cases tried. (41) On the other hand, it is easy to reckon up what a number of advantages the Athenian People derive from the practice impugned. In the first place, there is the steady receipt of salaries throughout the year (42) derived from the court fees. (43) Next, it enables them to manage the affairs of the allied states while seated at home without the expense of naval expeditions. Thirdly, they thus preserve the partisans of the democracy, and ruin her opponents in the law courts. Whereas, supposing the several allied states tried their cases at home, being inspired by hostility to Athens, they would destroy those of their own citizens whose friendship to the Athenian People was most marked. But besides all this the democracy derives the following advantages from hearing the cases of her allies in Athens. In the first place, the one per cent (44) levied in Piraeus is increased to the profit of the state; again, the owner of a lodging-house (45) does better, and so, too, the owner of a pair of beasts, or of slaves to be let out on hire; (46) again, heralds and criers (47) are a class of people who fare better owing to the sojourn of foreigners at Athens. Further still, supposing the allies had not to resort to Athens for the hearing of cases, only the official representative of the imperial state would be held in honour, such as the general, or trierarch, or ambassador. Whereas now every single individual among the allies is forced to pay flattery to the People of Athens because he knows that he must betake himself to Athens and win or lose (48) his case at the bar, not of any stray set of judges, but of the sovereign People itself, such being the law and customat Athens. He is compelled to behave as a suppliant (49) in the courts of justice, and when some juryman comes into court, to grasp his hand. For this reason, therefore, the allies find themselves more and more in the position of slaves to the people of Athens.

(40) Grote, "H. G." vi. 61.

(41) See Isocr. "Panath." 245 D.

(42) See Arist. "Clouds," 1196; Demosth. "c. Timoc." 730.

(43) For the "Prytaneia," see Aristot. "Pol." ii. 12, 4. "Ephialtes and Pericles curtailed the privileges of the Areopagus, Pericles converted the Courts of Law into salaried bodies, and so each succeeding demagogue outdid his predecessor in the privileges he conferred upon the commons, until the present democracy was the result" (Welldon). "The writer of this passage clearly intended to class Pericles among the demagogues. He judges him in the same deprecatory spirit as Plato in the 'Gorgias,' pp. 515, 516."—Jowett, "Pol. of Aristot." vol. ii. p. 101. But see Aristot. "Constitution of Athens," ch. xxv., a portion of the newly-discovered treatise, which throws light on an obscure period in the history of Athens; and Mr. Kenyon's note ad loc.; and Mr. Macan's criticism, "Journal of Hellenic Studies," vol. xii. No. 1.

(44) For the {ekatoste}, see Thuc. vii. 28, in reference to the year B.C. 416; Arist. "Wasps," 658; "Frogs," 363.

(45) See Boeckh, "P. E. A." I. xii. p. 65 (Eng. trans.); I. xxiv. p. 141.

(46) See "Revenues," iv. 20, p. 338; Jebb, "Theophr. Char." xxvi. 16.

(47) For these functionaries, see Jebb, op. cit. xvi. 10.

(48) Lit. "pay or get justice."

(49) Se Arist. "Wasps," 548 foll.; Grote, "H. G." v. 520 note; Newman, op. cit. i. 383.

Furthermore, owing to the possession of property beyond the limits of Attica, (50) and the exercise of magistracies which take them into regions beyond the frontier, they and their attendants have insensibly acquired the art of navigation. (51) A man who is perpetually voyaging is forced to handle the oar, he and his domestics alike, and to learn the terms familiar in seamanship. Hence a stock of skilful mariners is produced, bred upon a wide experience of voyaging and practice. They have learnt their business, some in piloting a small craft, others a merchant vessel, whilst others have been drafted off from these for service on a ship-of-war. So that the majority of them are able to row the moment they set foot on board a vessel, having been in a state of preliminary practice all their lives.

(50) See "Mem." II. viii. 1.

(51) See "Hell." VII. i. 4.

II

As to the heavy infantry, an arm the deficiency of which at Athens is well recognised, this is how the matter stands. They recognise the fact that, in reference to the hostile power, they are themselves inferior, and must be, even if their heavy infantry were more numerous. (1) But relatively to the allies, who bring in the tribute, their strength even on land is enormous. And they are persuaded that their heavy infantry is sufficient for all purposes, provided they retain this superiority. (2) Apart from all else, to a certain extent fortune must be held responsible for the actual condition. The subjects of a power which is dominant by land have it open to them to form contingents from several small states and to muster in force for battle. But with the subjects of a naval power it is different. As far as they are groups of islanders it is impossible for their states to meet together for united action, for the sea lies between them, and the dominant power is master of the sea. And even if it were possible for them to assemble in some single island unobserved, they would only do so to perish by famine. And as to the states subject to Athens which are not islanders, but situated on the continent, the larger are held in check by need (3) and the small ones absolutely by fear, since there is no state in existence which does not depend upon imports and exports, and these she will forfeit if she does not lend a willing ear to those who are masters by sea. In the next place, a power dominant by sea can do certain things which a land power is debarred from doing; as for instance, ravage the territory of a superior, since it is always possible to coast along to some point, where either there is no hostile force to deal with or merely a small body; and in case of an advance in force on the part of the enemy they can take to their ships and sail away. Such a performance is attended with less difficulty than that experienced by the relieving force on land. (4) Again, it is open to a power so dominating by sea to leave its own territory and sail off on as long a voyage as you please. Whereas the land power cannot place more than a few days' journey between itself and its own territory, for marches are slow affairs; and it is not possible for an army on the march to have food supplies to last for any great length of time. Such an army must either march through friendly territory or it must force a way by victory in battle. The voyager meanwhile has it in his power to disembark at any point where he finds himself in superior force, or, at the worst, to coast by until he reaches either a friendly district or an enemy too weak to resist. Again, those diseases to which the fruits of the earth are liable as visitations from heaven fall severely on a land power, but are scarcely felt by the navel power, for such sicknesses do not visit the whole earth everywhere at once. So that the ruler of the sea can get in supplies from a thriving district. And if one may descend to more trifling particulars, it is to this same lordship of the sea that the Athenians owe the discovery, in the first place, of many of the luxuries of life through intercourse with other countries. So that the choice things of Sicily and Italy, of Cyprus and Egypt and Lydia, of Pontus or Peloponnese, or wheresoever else it be, are all swept, as it were, into one centre, and all owing, as I say, to their maritime empire. And again, in process of listening to every form of speech, (5) they have selected this from one place and that from another—for themselves. So much so that while the rest of the Hellenes employ (6) each pretty much their own peculiar mode of speech, habit of life, and style of dress, the Athenians have adopted a composite type, (7) to which all sections of Hellas, and the foreigner alike, have contributed.

(1) Reading after Kirchhoff, {ettous ge... kan ei meizon en, ton dia k.t.l.} See Thuc. i. 143; Isocr. "de Pace," 169 A; Plut. "Them." 4 (Clough, i. 235).

(2) Lit. "they are superior to their allies."

(3) Reading with Kirchhoff, {dia khreian... dia deos}.

(4) Or, "the army marching along the seaboard to the rescue."

(5) Or, "a variety of dialects."

(6) Or, "maintain somewhat more."

(7) Or, "have contracted a mixed style, bearing traces of Hellenic and foreign influence alike." See Mahaffy, "Hist. of Greek Lit." vol. ii. ch. x. p. 257 (1st ed.); cf. Walt Whitman, "Preface to" original edition of "Leaves of Grass," p. 29—"The English language befriends the grand American expression: it is brawny enough and limber and full enough, on the tough stock of a race, who through all change of circumstances was never without the idea of a political liberty, which is the animus of all liberty; it has attracted the terms of daintier and gayer and subtler and more elegant tongues."

As regards sacrifices and temples and festivals and sacred enclosures, the

People sees that it is not possible for every poor citizen to do sacrifice and hold festival, or to set up (8) temples and to inhabit a large and beautiful city. But it has hit upon a means of meeting the difficulty. They sacrifice—that is, the whole state sacrifices—at the public cost a large number of victims; but it is the People that keeps holiday and distributes the victims by lot amongst its members. Rich men have in some cases private gymnasia and baths with dressing-rooms, (9) but the People takes care to have built at the public cost (10) a number of palaestras, dressing-rooms, and bathing establishments for its own special use, and the mob gets the benefit of the majority of these, rather than the select few or the well-to-do.

(8) Reading with Kirchhoff, {istasthai}.

(9) See Jebb, "Theophr. Char." vii. 18, p. 202.

(10) Reading with Kirchhoff, {demosia}.

As to wealth, the Athenians are exceptionally placed with regard to Hellenic and foreign communities alike, (11) in their ability to hold it. For, given that some state or other is rich in timber for shipbuilding, where is it to find a market (12) for the product except by persuading the ruler of the sea? Or, suppose the wealth of some state or other to consist of iron, or may be of bronze, (13) or of linen yarn, where will it find a market except by permission of the supreme maritime power? Yet these are the very things, you see, which I need for my ships. Timber I must have from one, and from another iron, from a third bronze, from a fourth linen yarn, from a fifth wax, etc. Besides which they will not suffer their antagonists in those parts (14) to carry these products elsewhither, or they will cease to use the sea. Accordingly I, without one stroke of labour, extract from the land and possess all these good things, thanks to my supremacy on the sea; whilst not a single other state possesses the two of them. Not timber, for instance, and yarn together, the same city. But where yarn is abundant, the soil will be light and devoid of timber. And in the same way bronze and iron will not be products of the same city. And so for the rest, never two, or at best three, in one state, but one thing here and another thing there. Moreover, above and beyond what has been said, the coast-line of every mainland presents, either some jutting promontory, or adjacent island, or narrow strait of some sort, so that those who are masters of the sea can come to moorings at one of these points and wreak vengeance (15) on the inhabitants of the mainland.

(11) Or, "they have a practical monopoly."

(12) Or, "how is it to dispose of the product?"

(13) Or, "coppert."

(14) Reading {ekei}. For this corrupt passage see L. Dindorf, ad. loc.; also Boeckh, "P. E. A." I. ix. p. 55. Perhaps (as my friend Mr. J. R. Mozley suggests) the simplest supposition is to suppose

that there is an ellipsis before {e ou khresontai te thalatte}: thus, "Besides which they will not suffer their antagonists to transport goods to countries outside Attica; they must yield, or they shall not have the use of the sea."

(15) {lobasthai}. This "poetical" word comes to mean "harry," "pillage," in the common dialect.

There is just one thing which the Athenians lack. Supposing that they were the inhabitants of an island, (16) and were still, as now, rulers of the sea, they would have had it in their power to work whatever mischief they liked, and to suffer no evil in return (as long as they kept command of the sea), neither the ravaging of their territory nor the expectation of an enemy's approach. Whereas at present the farming portion of the community and the wealthy landowners are ready (17) to cringe before the enemy overmuch, whilst the People, knowing full well that, come what may, not one stock or stone of their property will suffer, nothing will be cut down, nothing burnt, lives in freedom from alarm, without fawning at the enemy's approach. Besides this, there is another fear from which they would have been exempt in an island home—the apprehension of the city being at any time betrayed by their oligarchs (18) and the gates thrown open, and an enemy bursting suddenly in. How could incidents like these have taken place if an island had been their home? Again, had they inhabited an island there would have been no stirring of sedition against the people; whereas at present, in the event of faction, those who set it in foot base their hopes of success on the introduction of an enemy by land. But a people inhabiting an island would be free from all anxiety on that score. Since, however, they did not chance to inhabit an island from the first, what they now do is this—they deposit their property in the islands, (19) trusting to their command of the sea, and they suffer the soil of Aticca to be ravaged without a sigh. To expend pity on that, they know, would be to deprive themselves of other blessings still more precious. (20)

(16) See Thuc. i. 143. Pericles says: "Reflect, if we were islanders, who would be more invulnerable? Let us imagine that we are."

(17) Or, "are the more ready to cringe." See, for the word {uperkhontai}, "Pol. Lac." viii. 2; Plat. "Crit." 53 E; Rutherford, "New Phrynichus," p. 110.

(18) Or, "by the minority"; or, "by a handful of people."

(19) As they did during the Peloponnesian war; and earlier still, before the battle of Salamis, in the case of that one island.

(20) Or, "but mean the forfeiture of others."

Further, states oligarchically governed are forced to ratify their alliances and solemn oaths, and if they fail to abide by their contracts, the offence, by whomsoever committed, (21) lies nominally at the door of the oligarchs who entered upon the contract. But in the case of engagements entered into by a democracy it is open to the People to throw the blame on the single individual who spoke in favour of some measure, or put it to the vote, and to maintain to the rest of the world, "I was not present, nor do I approve of the terms of the agreement." Inquiries are made in a full meeting of the People, and should any of these things be disapproved of, it can at once discover ten thousand excuses to avoid doing whatever they do not wish. And if any mischief should spring out of any resolutions which the People has passed in council, the People can readily shift the blame from its own shoulders. "A handful of oligarchs (22) acting against the interests of the People have ruined us." But if any good result ensue, they, the People, at once take the credit of that to themselves.

(21) Reading {uph otououn adikeitai onomati upo ton oligon}, which I suggest as a less violent emendation of this corrupt passage than any I have seen; or, reading with Sauppe, {uph otou adikei anomeitai apo ton oligon}, "the illegality lies at the door of."

(22) Or, "a few insignificant fellows."

In the same spirit it is not allowed to caricature on the comic stage (23) or otherwise libel the People, because (24) they do not care to hear themselves ill spoken of. But if any one has a desire to satirise his neighbour he has full leave to do so. And this because they are well aware that, as a general rule, this person caricatured (25) does not belong to the People, or the masses. He is more likely to be some wealthy or well-born person, or man of means and influence. In fact, but few poor people and of the popular stamp incur the comic lash, or if they do they have brought it on themselves by excessive love of meddling or some covetous self-seeking at the expense of the People, so that no particular annoyance is felt at seeing such folk satirised.

(23) See Grote, "H. G." viii. 446, especially p. 449, "growth and development of comedy at Athens"; Curtius, "H. G." iii. pp. 242, 243; Thirlwall, "H. G." ch. xviii. vol. iii. p. 42.

(24) Or, more lit. "it would not do for the People to hear," etc.

(25) Or, "the butt of comedy."

What, then, I venture to assert is, that the People of Athens has no difficulty in recognising which of its citizens are of the better sort and which the opposite. (26) And so recognising those who are serviceable and advantageous (27) to itself, even though they be base, the People loves them; but the good folk they are disposed rather to hate. This virtue of theirs, the People holds, is not engrained in their nature for any good to itself, but rather for its injury. In direct opposition to this, there are some persons who, being
(28) born of the People, are yet by natural instinct not commoners. For my part I pardon the People its own democracy, as, indeed, it is pardonable in any one to do good to himself. (29) But the man who, not being himself one of the People, prefers to live in a state democratically governed rather than in an oligarchical state may be said to smooth his own path towards iniquity. He

knows that a bad man has a better chance of slipping through the fingers of justice in a democratic than in an oligarchical state.

(26) Or, "and which are good for nothing."

(27) Or, "its own friends and supporters."

(28) Reading {ontes} or (if {gnontes}), "who, recognising the nature of the People, have no popular leaning." Gutschmidt conj. {enioi egguoi ontes}, i.e. Pericles.

(29) On the principle that "the knee is nearer than the shin-bone," {gonu knemes}, or, as we say, "charity begins at home."

III

I repeat that my position concerning the polity of the Athenians is this: the type (1) of polity is not to my taste, but given that a democratic form of government has been agreed upon, they do seem to me to go the right way to preserve the democracy by the adoption of the particular type (2) which I have set forth.

(1) Or, "manner."

(2) Or, "manner."

But there are other objections brought, as I am aware, against the Athenians, by certain people, and to this effect. It not seldom happens, they tell us, that a man is unable to transact a piece of business with the senate or the People, even if he sit waiting a whole year. Now this does happen at Athens, and for no other reason save that, owing to the immense mass of affairs they are unable to work off all the business on hand, and dismiss the applicants. And how in the world should they be able, considering in the first place, that they, the Athenians, have more festivals (3) to celebrate than any other state throughout the length and breadth of Hellas? (During these festivals, of course, the transaction of any sort of affairs of state is still more out of the question.) (4) In the next place, only consider the number of cases they have to decide—what with private suits and public causes and scrutinies of accounts, etc., more than the whole of the rest of mankind put together; while the senate has multifarious points to advise upon concerning peace and war, (5) concerning ways and means, concerning the framing and passing of laws, (6) and concerning the thousand and one matters affecting the state perpetually occurring, and endless questions touching the allies; besides the receipt of the tribute, the superintendence of dockyards and temples, etc. Can, I ask again, any one find it at all surprising that, with all these affairs on their hands, they are unequal to doing business with all the world?

(3) See Arist. "Wasps," 661.

(4) This sentence is perhaps a gloss.

(5) Or, "about the war," {peri tou polemou}.

(6) See Thirlwall, ch. xxxii. vol. iv. p. 221, note 3.

But some people tell us that if the applicant will only address himself to the senate or the People with a fee in his hand he will do a good stroke of business. And for my part I am free to confess to these gainsayers that a good many things may be done at Athens by dint of money; and I will add, that a good many more still might be done, if the money flowed still more freely and from more pockets. One thing, however, I know full well, that as to transacting with every one of these applicants all he wants, the state could not do it, not even if all the gold and silver in the world were the inducement offered.

Here are some of the cases which have to be decided on. Some one fails to fit out a ship: judgement must be given. Another puts up a building on apiece of public land: again judgement must be given. Or, to take another class of cases: adjudication has to be made between the choragi for the Dionysia, the Thargelia, the Panathenaea, year after year. ((7) And again in behalf of the gymnasiarchs a similar adjudication for the Panathenaea, the Prometheia, and the Hephaestia, also year after year.) Also as between the trierarchs, four hundred of whom are appointed each year, of these, too, any who choose must have their cases adjudicated on, year after year. But that is not all. There are various magistrates to examine and approve (8) and decide between; there are orphans (9) whose status must be examined; and guardians of prisoners to appoint. These, be it borne in mind, are all matters of yearly occurrence; while at intervals there are exemptions and abstentions from military service (10) which call for adjudication, or in connection with some other extraordinary misdemeanour, some case of outrage and violence of an exceptional character, or some charge of impiety. A whole string of others I simply omit; I am content to have named the most important part with the exception of the assessments of tribute which occur, as a rule, at intervals of five years. (11)

(7) Adopting the emendation of Kirchhoff, who inserts the sentence in brackets. For the festivals in question, see "Dict. of Antiq." "Lampadephoria"; C. R. Kenney, "Demosth. against Leptines," etc., App. vi.

(8) For the institution called the {dokimasia}, see Aristot. "Constitution of Athens," ch. lv.

(9) See Dem. "against Midias," 565, 17; "against Apholus" (1), 814, 20.

(10) See Lys. "Or." xiv. and xv.

(11) See Grote, "H. G." vi. p. 48; Thuc. vii. 78; i. 96; Arist. "Wasps," 707; Aristot. "Pol." v. 8.

I put it to you, then: can any one suppose that all, or any, of these may dispense with adjudication? (12) If so, will any one say which ought, and which ought not, to be adjudicated on, there and then? If, on the other hand, we are forced to admit that these are all fair cases for adjudication, it follows of necessity that they should be decided during the twelve-month; since even now the boards of judges sitting right through the year are powerless to stay the tide of evildoing by reason of the multitude of the people.

(12) Reading with Kirchhoff. Cf. for {oiesthai khre}, "Hell." VI. iv. 23; "Cyr." IV. ii. 28.

So far so good. (13) "But," some one will say, "try the cases you certainly must, but lessen the number of the judges." But if so, it follows of necessity that unless the number of courts themselves are diminished in number there will only be a few judges sitting in each court, (14) with the further consequence that in dealing with so small a body of judges it will be easier for a litigant to present an invulnerable front (15) to the court, and to bribe (16) the whole body, to the great detriment of justice. (17)

(13) See Grote, "H. G." v. 514, 520; Machiavelli, "Disc. s. Livio," i. 7.

(14) Reading with Sauppe, {anagke toinun, ean me} (for the vulgate {ean men oliga k.t.l.}) {oliga poiontai dikasteria, oligoi en ekasto esontai to dikasterio}. Or, adopting Weiske's emendation, {ean men polla poiontai dikasteria k.t.l.} Translate, "Then, if by so doing they manage to multiply the law courts, there will be only a few judges sitting," etc.

(15) Or, as Liddell and Scott, "to prepare all his tricks."

(16) {sundekasoi}, "to bribe in the lump." This is Schneider's happy emendation of the MS. {sundikasai}; see Demosthenes, 1137, 1.

(17) Reading {oste}, lit. "so as to get a far less just judgment."

But besides this we cannot escape the conclusion that the Athenians have their festivals to keep, during which the courts cannot sit. (18) As a matter of fact these festivals are twice as numerous as those of any other people. But I will reckon them as merely equal to those of the state which has the fewest.

(18) Lit. "it is not possible to give judgment"; or, "for juries to sit."

This being so, I maintain that it is not possible for business affairs at Athens to stand on any very different footing from the present, except to some slight extent, by adding here and deducting there. Any large modification is out of the question, short of damaging the democracy itself. No doubt many expedients might be discovered for improving the constitution, but if the problem be to discover some adequate means of improving the constitution, while at the same time the democracy is to remain intact, I say it is not easy to do this, except, as I have just stated, to the extent of some trifling addition here or deduction there.

There is another point in which it is sometimes felt that the Athenians are ill advised, in their adoption, namely, of the less respectable party, in a state divided by faction. But if so, they do it advisedly. If they chose the more respectable, they would be adopting those whose views and interests differ from their own, for there is no state in which the best element is friendly to the people. It is the worst element which in every state favours the democracy —on the principle that like favours like. (19) It is simple enough then. The

Athenians choose what is most akin to themselves. Also on every occasion on which they have attempted to side with the better classes, it has not faredwell with them, but within a short interval the democratic party has been enslaved, as for instance in Boeotia; (20) or, as when they chose the aristocrats of the Milesians, and within a short time these revolted and cut the people to pieces; or, as when they chose the Lacedaemonians as against the Messenians, and within a short time the Lacedaemonians subjugated the Messenians and went to war against Athens.

(19) I.e. "birds of a feather."

(20) The references are perhaps (1) to the events of the year 447 B.C., see Thuc. i. 113; cf. Aristot. "Pol." v. 3, 5; (2) to 440 B.C., Thuc. i. 115; Diod. xii. 27, 28; Plut. "Pericl." c. 24; (3) to those of 464 B.C., followed by 457 B.C., Thuc. i. 102; Plut. "Cimon," c. 16; and Thuc. i. 108.

I seem to overhear a retort, "No one, of course, is deprived of his civil rights at Athens unjustly." My answer is, that there are some who are unjustly deprived of their civil rights, though the cases are certainly rare. But it will take more than a few to attack the democracy at Athens, since you may take it as an established fact, it is not the man who has lost his civil rights justly that takes the matter to heart, but the victims, if any, of injustice. But how in the world can any one imagine that many are in a state of civil disability at Athens, where the People and the holders of office are one and the same? It is from iniquitous exercise of office, from iniquity exhibited either in speech or action, and the like circumstances, that citizens are punished with deprivation of civil rights in Athens. Due reflection on these matters will serve to dispel the notion that there is any danger at Athens from persons visited with disenfranchisement.

THE POLITY OF THE LACEDAEMONIANS

I

I recall the astonishment with which I (1) first noted the unique position (2) of Sparta amongst the states of Hellas, the relatively sparse population, (3) and at the same time the extraordinary power and prestige of the community. I was puzzled to account for the fact. It was only when I came to consider the peculiar institutions of the Spartans that my wonderment ceased. Or rather, it is transferred to the legislator who gave them those laws, obedience to which has been the secret of their prosperity. This legislator, Lycurgus, I must needs admire, and hold him to have been one of the wisest of mankind. Certainly he was no servile imitator of other states. It was by a stroke of invention rather, and on a pattern much in opposition to the commonly-accepted one, that he brought his fatherland to this pinnacle of prosperity.

(1) See the opening words of the "Cyrop." and of the "Symp."

(2) Or, "the phenomenal character." See Grote, "H. G." ix. 320 foll.; Newman, "Pol. Arist." i. 202.

(3) See Herod. vii. 234; Aristot. "Pol." ii. 9, 14 foll.; Muller, "Dorians," iii. 10 (vol. i. p. 203, Eng. tr.)

Take for example—and it is well to begin at the beginning (4)—the whole topic of the begetting and rearing of children. Throughout the rest of the world the young girl, who will one day become a mother (and I speak of those who may be held to be well brought up), is nurtured on the plainest food attainable, with the scantiest addition of meat or other condiments; whilst as to wine they train them either to total abstinence or to take it highly diluted with water. And in imitation, as it were, of the handicraft type, since the majority of artificers are sedentary, (5) we, the rest of the Hellenes, are content that our girls should sit quietly and work wools. That is all we demand of them. But how are we to expect that women nurtured in this fashion should produce a splendid offspring?

(4) Cf. a fragment of Critias cited by Clement, "Stromata," vi. p. 741, 6; Athen. x. 432, 433; see "A Fragment of Xenophon" (?), ap. Stob. "Flor." 88. 14, translated by J. Hookham Frere, "Theognis Restitutus," vol. i. 333; G. Sauppe, "Append. de Frag. Xen." p. 293; probably by Antisthenes (Bergk. ii. 497).

(5) Or, "such technical work is for the most part sedentary."

Lycurgus pursued a different path. Clothes were things, he held, the furnishing of which might well enough be left to female slaves. And, believing that the highest function of a free woman was the bearing of children, in the first place he insisted on the training of the body as incumbent no less on the female than the male; and in pursuit of the same idea instituted rival contests in running and feats of strength for women as for men. His belief was that where both parents were strong their progeny would be found to be more vigorous.

And so again after marriage. In view of the fact that immoderate intercourse is elsewhere permitted during the earlier period of matrimony, he adopted a principle directly opposite. He laid it down as an ordinance that a man should be ashamed to be seen visiting the chamber of his wife, whether going in or coming out. When they did meet under such restraint the mutual longing of these lovers could not but be increased, and the fruit which might spring from such intercourse would tend to be more robust than theirs whose affections are cloyed by satiety. By a farther step in the same direction he refused to allow marriages to be contracted (6) at any period of life according to the fancy of the parties concerned. Marriage, as he ordained it, must only take place in the prime of bodily vigour, (7) this too being, as he believed, a condition conducive to the production of healthy offspring. Or again, to meet the case which might occur of an old man (8) wedded to a young wife. Considering the jealous watch which such husbands are apt to keep over their wives, he introduced a directly opposite custom; that is to say, he made it incumbent on the aged husband to introduce some one whose qualities, physical and moral, he admired, to play the husband's part and to beget him children. Or again, in the case of a man who might not desire to live with a wife permanently, but yet might still be anxious to have children of his own worthy the name, the lawgiver laid down a law (9) in his behalf. Such a one might select some woman, the wife of some man, well born herself and blest with fair offspring, and, the sanction and consent of her husband first obtained, raise up children for himself through her.

(6) "The bride to be wooed and won." The phrase {agesthai} perhaps points to some primitive custom of capturing and carrying off the bride, but it had probably become conventional.

(7) Cf. Plut. "Lycurg," 15 (Clough, i. 101). "In their marriages the husband carried off his bride by a sort of force; nor were their brides ever small and of tender years, but in their full bloom and ripeness."

(8) Cf. Plut. "Lycurg." 15 (Clough, i. 103).

(9) Or, "established a custom to suit the case."

These and many other adaptations of a like sort the lawgiver sanctioned. As, for instance, at Sparta a wife will not object to bear the burden of a double establishment, (10) or a husband to adopt sons as foster-brothers of his own children, with a full share in his family and position, but possessing no claim to his wealth and property.

(10) Cf. Plut. "Comp. of Numa with Lycurgus," 4; "Cato mi." 25

(Clough, i. 163; iv. 395).

So opposed to those of the rest of the world are the principles which Lycurgus devised in reference to the production of children. Whether they enabled him to provide Sparta with a race of men superior to all in size and strength I leave to the judgment of whomsoever it may concern.

II

With this exposition of the customs in connection with the birth of children, I wish now to explain the systems of education in fashion here andelsewhere. Throughout the rest of Hellas the custom on the part of those who claim to educate their sons in the best way is as follows. As soon as the children are of an age to understand what is said to them they are immediately placed under the charge of Paidagogoi (1) (or tutors), who are also attendants, and sent off to the school of some teacher to be taught "grammar," "music," and the concerns of the palestra. (2) Besides this they are given shoes (3) to wear which tend to make their feet tender, and their bodies are enervated by various changes of clothing. And as for food, the only measure recognised is that which is fixed by appetite.

(1) = "boy-leaders." Cf. St. Paul, "Ep. Gal." iii. 24; The Law was our schoolmaster to bring us unto Christ.

(2) Cf. Plato, "Alc. maj." 106 E; "Theages," 122 E; Aristot. "Pol." viii. 3.

(3) Or, "sandals."

But when we turn to Lycurgus, instead of leaving it to each member of the state privately to appoint a slave to be his son's tutor, he set over the young Spartans a public guardian, the Paidonomos (4) or "pastor," to give them his proper title, (5) with complete authority over them. This guardian was selected from those who filled the highest magistracies. He had authority to hold musters of the boys, (6) and as their overseer, in case of any misbehaviour, to chastise severely. The legislator further provided his pastor with a body of youths in the prime of life, and bearing whips, (7) to inflict punishment when necessary, with this happy result that in Sparta modestyand obedience ever go hand in hand, nor is there lack ofeither.

(4) = "boyherd."

(5) Cf. Plut. "Lycurg." 17 (Clough, i. 107); Aristot. "Pol." iv. 15, 13; vii. 17, 5.

(6) Or, "assemble the boys in flocks."

(7) {mastigophoroi} = "flagellants."

Instead of softening their feet with shoe or sandal, his rule was to make them hardy through going barefoot. (8) This habit, if practised, would, as he believed, enable them to scale heights more easily and clamber down precipices with less danger. In fact, with his feet so trained the young Spartan would leap and spring and run faster unshod than another shod in the ordinary way.

(8) Cf. Plut. "Lycurg." 16 (Clough, i. 106).

Instead of making them effeminate with a variety of clothes, his rule was to habituate them to a single garment the whole year through, thinking that so they would be better prepared to withstand the variations of heat and cold.

Again, as regards food, according to his regulation the Eiren, (9) or head of the flock, must see that his messmates gathered to the club meal, (10) with such moderate food as to avoid that heaviness (11) which is engendered by repletion, and yet not to remain altogether unacquainted with the pains of penurious living. His belief was that by such training in boyhood they would be better able when occasion demanded to continue toiling on an empty stomach. They would be all the fitter, if the word of command were given, to remain on the stretch for a long time without extra dieting. The craving for luxuries (12) would be less, the readiness to take any victual set before them greater, and, in general, the regime would be found more healthy. (13) Under it he thought the lads would increase in stature and shape into finer men, since, as he maintained, a dietary which gave suppleness to the limbs must be more conducive to both ends than one which added thickness to the bodily parts by feeding. (14)

(9) For the Eiren, see Plut. "Lycurg." (Clough, i. 107).

(10) Reading {sumboleuein} (for the vulg. {sumbouleuein}). The emendation is now commonly adopted. For the word itself, see L. Dindorf, n. ad loc., and Schneider. {sumbolon} = {eranos} or club meal. Perhaps we ought to read {ekhontas} instead of {ekhonta}.

(11) See Plut. "Lycurg." 17 (Clough, i. 108).

(12) Lit. "condiments," such as "meat," "fish," etc. See "Cyrop." I. ii. 8.

(13) Or, "and in general they would live more healthily and increase in stature."

(14) See L. Dindorf's emendation of this corrupt passage, n. ad loc. (based upon Plut. "Lycurg." 17 and Ps. Plut. "Moral." 237), {kai eis mekos d' an auxanesthai oeto kai eueidesterous} vel {kallious gignesthai, pros amphotera ton radina ta somata poiousan trophen mallon sullambanein egesamenos e ten diaplatunousan}. Otherwise I would suggest to read {kai eis mekos an auxanesthai ten (gar) radina... egesato k.t.l.}, which is closer to the vulgate, and gives nearly the same sense.

On the other hand, in order to guard against a too great pinch of starvation, though he did not actually allow the boys to help themselves without further trouble to what they needed more, he did give them permission to steal (15) this thing or that in the effort to alleviate their hunger. It was not of course from any real difficulty how else to supply them with nutriment that he left it to them to provide themselves by this crafty method. Nor can I conceive that any one will so misinterpret the custom. Clearly its explanation lies in the fact that he who would live the life of a robber must forgo sleep by night, and in the daytime he must employ shifts and lie in ambuscade; he must prepare and make ready his scouts, and so forth, if he is to succeed in capturing the quarry. (16)

(15) See "Anab." IV. vi. 14.

(16) For the institution named the {krupteia}, see Plut. "Lycurg." 28 (Clough, i. 120); Plato, "Laws," i. 633 B; for the {klopeia}, ib. vii. 823 E; Isocr. "Panathen." 277 B.

It is obvious, I say, that the whole of this education tended, and was intended, to make the boys craftier and more inventive in getting in supplies, whilst at the same time it cultivated their warlike instincts. An objector may retort: "But if he thought it so fine a feat to steal, why did he inflict all those blows on the unfortunate who was caught?" My answer is: for the self-same reason which induces people, in other matters which are taught, to punish the mal-performance of a service. So they, the Lacedaemonians, visit penalties on the boy who is detected thieving as being but a sorry bungler in the art. So to steal as many cheeses as possible (off the shrine of Orthia (17)) was a feat to be encouraged; but, at the same moment, others were enjoined to scourge the thief, which would point a moral not obscurely, that by pain endured for a brief season a man may earn the joyous reward of lasting glory. (18) Herein, too, it is plainly shown that where speed is requisite the sluggard will win for himself much trouble and scant good.

(17) I.e. "Artemis of the Steep"—a title connecting the goddess with Mount Orthion or Orthosion. See Pausan. VIII. xxiii. 1; and for the custom, see Themistius, "Or." 21, p. 250 A. The words have perhaps got out of their right place. See Schneider's Index, s.v.

(18) See Plut. "Lycurg." 18; "Morals," 239 C; "Aristid." 17; Cic. "Tusc." ii. 14.

Furthermore, and in order that the boys should not want a ruler, even in case the pastor (19) himself were absent, he gave to any citizen who chanced to be present authority to lay upon them injunctions for their good, and to chastise them for any trespass committed. By so doing he created in the boys of Sparta a most rare modesty and reverence. And indeed there is nothing which, whether as boys or men, they respect more highly than the ruler. Lastly, and with the same intention, that the boys must never be reft of a ruler, even if by chance there were no grown man present, he laid down the rule that in such a case the most active of the Leaders or Prefects (20) was to become ruler for the nonce, each of his own division. The conclusion being that under no circumstances whatever are the boys of Sparta destitute of one to rule them.

(19) Lit. "Paidonomos."

(20) Lit. "Eirens."

I ought, as it seems to me, not to omit some remark on the subject of boy attachments, (21) it being a topic in close connection with that of boyhood and the training of boys.

(21) See Plut. "Lycurg." 17 (Clough, i. 109).

We know that the rest of the Hellenes deal with this relationship in different ways, either after the manner of the Boeotians, (22) where man and boy are intimately united by a bond like that of wedlock, or after the manner of the Eleians, where the fruition of beauty is an act of grace; whilst there are others who would absolutely debar the lover from all conversation (23) and discourse with the beloved.

(22) See Xen. "Symp." viii. 34; Plato, "Symp." 182 B (Jowett, II. p. 33).

(23) {dialegesthai} came to mean philosophic discussion and debate. Is the author thinking of Socrates? See "Mem." I. ii. 35; IV. v. 12.

Lycurgus adopted a system opposed to all of these alike. Given that some one, himself being all that a man ought to be, should in admiration of a boy's soul (24) endeavour to discover in him a true friend without reproach, and to consort with him—this was a relationship which Lycurgus commended, and indeed regarded as the noblest type of bringing up. But if, as was evident, it was not an attachment to the soul, but a yearning merely towards the body, he stamped this thing as foul and horrible; and with this result, to the credit of Lycurgus be it said, that in Lacedaemon the relationship of lover and beloved is like that of parent and child or brother and brother where carnal appetite is in abeyance.

(24) See Xen. "Symp." viii. 35; Plut. "Lycurg." 18.

That this, however, which is the fact, should be scarcely credited in some quarters does not surprise me, seeing that in many states the laws (25) do not oppose the desires in question.

(25) I.e. "law and custom."

I have now described the two chief methods of education in vogue; that is to say, the Lacedaemonian as contrasted with that of the rest of Hellas, and I leave it to the judgment of him whom it may concern, which of the two has produced the finer type of men. And by finer I mean the better disciplined, the more modest and reverential, and, in matters where self-restraint is a virtue, the more continent.

III

Coming to the critical period at which a boy ceases to be a boy and becomes a youth, (1) we find that it is just then that the rest of the world proceed to emancipate their children from the private tutor and the schoolmaster, and, without substituting any further ruler, are content to launch them into absolute independence.

(1) {eis to meirakiousthai}, "with reference to hobbledehoy-hood." Cobet erases the phrase as post-Xenophontine.

Here, again, Lycurgus took an entirely opposite view of the matter. This, if observation might be trusted, was the season when the tide of animal spirits flows fast, and the froth of insolence rises to the surface; when, too, the most violent appetites for divers pleasures, in serried ranks, invade (2) the mind. This, then, was the right moment at which to impose tenfold labours upon the growing youth, and to devise for him a subtle system of absorbing occupation. And by a crowning enactment, which said that "he who shrank from the duties imposed on him would forfeit henceforth all claim to the glorious honours of the state," he caused, not only the public authorities, but those personally interested (3) in the several companies of youths to take serious pains so that no single individual of them should by an act of craven cowardice find himself utterly rejected and reprobate within the body politic.

(2) Lit. "range themselves." For the idea, see "Mem." I. ii. 23; Swinburne, "Songs before Sunrise": Prelude, "Past youth where shoreward shallows are."

(3) Or, "the friends and connections."

Furthermore, in his desire to implant in their youthful souls a root of modesty he imposed upon these bigger boys a special rule. In the very streets they were to keep their two hands (4) within the folds of the cloak; they were to walk in silence and without turning their heads to gaze, now here, now there, but rather to keep their eyes fixed upon the ground before them. And hereby it would seem to be proved conclusively that, even in the matter of quiet bearing and sobriety, (5) the masculine type may claim greater strength than that which we attribute to the nature of women. At any rate, you might sooner expect a stone image to find voice than one of those Spartan youths; to divert the eyes of some bronze stature were less difficult. And as to quiet bearing, no bride ever stepped in bridal bower (6) with more natural modesty. Note them when they have reached the public table. (7) The plainest answer to the question asked—that is all you need expect to hear from their lips.

(4) See Cic. "pro Coelio," 5.

(5) See Plat. "Charmid." 159 B; Jowett, "Plato," I. 15.

(6) Longinus, {peri ups}, iv. 4, reading {ophthalmois} for {thalamois}, says: "Yet why speak of Timaeus, when even men like Xenophon and Plato, the very demigods of literature, though they had sat at the feet of Socrates, sometimes forget themselves in the pursuit of such pretty conceits? The former in his account of the Spartan Polity has these words: 'Their voice you would no more hear, than if they were of marble, their gaze is as immovable as if they were cast in bronze. You would deem them more modest than

the very maidens in their eyes.' To speak of the pupils of the eyes as modest maidens was a piece of absurdity becoming Amphicrates rather than Xenophon; and then what a strange notion to suppose that modesty is always without exception, expressed in the eye!"—H. L. Howell, "Longinus," p. 8. See "Spectator," No. 354.

(7) See Paus. VII. i. 8, the {phidition} or {philition}; "Hell." V. iv. 28.

IV

But if he was thus careful in the education of the stripling, (1) the Spartan lawgiver showed a still greater anxiety in dealing with those who had reached the prime of opening manhood; considering their immense importance to the city in the scale of good, if only they proved themselves the men they should be. He had only to look around to see what wherever the spirit of emulation (2) is most deeply seated, there, too, their choruses and gymnastic contests will present alike a far higher charm to eye and ear. And on the same principle he persuaded himself that he needed only to confront (3) his youthful warriors in the strife of valour, and with like result. They also, in their degree, might be expected to attain to some unknown height of manly virtue.

(1) See "Hell." V. iv. 32.

(2) Cf. "Cyrop." II. i. 22.

(3) Or, "pit face to face."

What method he adopted to engage these combatants I will now explain. It is on this wise. Their ephors select three men out of the whole body of the citizens in the prime of life. These three are named Hippagretai, or masters of the horse. Each of these selects one hundred others, being bound to explain for what reason he prefers in honour these and disapproves of those. The result is that those who fail to obtain the distinction are now at open war, not only with those who rejected them, but with those who were chosen in their stead; and they keep ever a jealous eye on one another to detect some slip of conduct contrary to the high code of honour there held customary. And so is set on foot that strife, in truest sense acceptable to heaven, and for the purposes of state most politic. It is a strife in which not only is the pattern of a brave man's conduct fully set forth, but where, too, each against other and in separate camps, the rival parties train for victory. One day the superiority shall be theirs; or, in the day of need, one and all to the last man, they will be ready to aid the fatherland with all their strength.

Necessity, moreover, is laid upon them to study a good habit of the body, coming as they do to blows with their fists for very strife's sake whenever they meet. Albeit, any one present has a right to separate the combatants, and, if obedience is not shown to the peacemaker, the Pastor of youth (4) hales the delinquent before the ephors, and the ephors inflict heavy damages, since they will have it plainly understood that rage must never override obedience to law.

(4) Lit. "the Paidonomos."

With regard to those who have already passed (5) the vigour of early manhood, and on whom the highest magistracies henceforth devolve, there is a like contrast. In Hellas generally we find that at this age the need of further attention to physical strength is removed, although the imposition of military service continues. But Lycurgus made it customary for that section of his citizens to regard hunting as the highest honour suited to their age; albeit, not to the exclusion of any public duty. (6) And his aim was that they might be equally able to undergo the fatigues of war with those in the prime of early manhood.

(5) Probably the {agathoergoi}, technically so called. See Herod. i. 67; Schneider, ap. Dindorf.

(6) Lit. "save only if some public duty intervened." See "Cyrop." I. ii.

V

The above is a fairly exhaustive statement of the institutions traceable to the legislation of Lycurgus in connection with the successive stages (1) of a citizen's life. It remains that I should endeavour to describe the style of living which he established for the whole body, irrespective of age. It will be understood that, when Lycurgus first came to deal with the question, the Spartans like the rest of the Hellenes, used to mess privately at home. Tracing more than half the current misdemeanours to this custom, (2) he was determined to drag his people out of holes and corners into the broad daylight, and so he invented the public mess-rooms. Whereby he expected at any rate to minimise the transgression of orders.

(1) Lit. "with each age."; see Plut. "Lycurg." 25; Hesychius, {s. u. irinies}; "Hell." VI. iv. 17; V. iv. 13.

(2) Reading after Cobet, {en touto}.

As to food, (3) his ordinance allowed them so much as, while not inducing repletion, should guard them from actual want. And, in fact, there are many exceptional (4) dishes in the shape of game supplied from the hunting field. Or, as a substitute for these, rich men will occasionally garnish the feast with wheaten loaves. So that from beginning to end, till the mess breaks up, the common board is never stinted for viands, nor yet extravagantly furnished.

(3) See Plut. "Lycurg." 12 (Clough, i. 97).

(4) {paraloga}, i.e. unexpected dishes, technically named {epaikla} (hors d'oeuvres), as we learn from Athenaeus, iv. 140, 141.

So also in the matter of drink. Whilst putting a stop to all unnecessary potations, detrimental alike to a firm brain and a steady gait, (5) he left them free to quench thirst when nature dictated (6); a method which would at once add to the pleasure whilst it diminished the danger of drinking. And indeed one may fairly ask how, on such a system of common meals, it would be possible for any one to ruin either himself or his family either through gluttony or wine-bibbing.

(5) Or, "apt to render brain and body alike unsteady."

(6) See "Agesilaus"; also "Mem." and "Cyrop."

This too must be borne in mind, that in other states equals in age, (7) for the most part, associate together, and such an atmosphere is little conducive to modesty. (8) Whereas in Sparta Lycurgus was careful so to blend the ages (9) that the younger men must benefit largely by the experience of the elder—an education in itself, and the more so since by custom of the country conversation at the common meal has reference to the honourable acts which this man or that man may have performed in relation to the state. The scene, in fact, but little lends itself to the intrusion of violence or drunken riot; ugly speech and ugly deeds alike are out of place. Amongst other good results obtained through this out-door system of meals may be mentioned these: There is the necessity of walking home when the meal is over, and a consequent anxiety not to be caught tripping under the influence of wine, since they all know of course that the supper-table must be presently abandoned, (10) and that they must move as freely in the dark as in the day, even the help of a torch (11) to guide the steps being forbidden to all on active service.

(7) Cf. Plat. "Phaedr." 240 C; {elix eklika terpei}, "Equals delight in equals."

(8) Or, "these gatherings for the most part consist of equals in age (young fellows), in whose society the virtue of modesty is least likely to display itself."

(9) See Plut. "Lycurg." 12 (Clough, i. 98).

(10) Or, "that they are not going to stay all night where they have supped."

(11) See Plut. "Lycurg." 12 (Clough, i. 99).

In connection with this matter, Lycurgus had not failed to observe the effect of equal amounts of food on different persons. The hardworking man has a good complexion, his muscles are well fed, he is robust and strong. The man who abstains from work, on the other hand, may be detected by his miserable appearance; he is blotched and puffy, and devoid of strength. This observation, I say, was not wasted on him. On the contrary, turning it over in his mind that any one who chooses, as a matter of private judgment, to devote himself to toil may hope to present a very creditable appearance physically, he enjoined upon the eldest for the time being in every gymnasium to see to it that the labours of the class were proportional to the meats. (12) And to my mind he was not out of his reckoning in this matter more than elsewhere. At any rate, it would be hard to discover a healthier or more completely developed human being, physically speaking, than the Spartan. Their gymnastic training, in fact, makes demands alike on the legs and arms and neck, (13) etc., simultaneously.

(12) I.e. "not inferior in excellence to the diet which they enjoyed." The reading here adopted I owe to Dr. Arnold Hug, {os me ponous auton elattous ton sition gignesthai}.

(13) See Plat. "Laws," vii. 796 A; Jowett, "Plato," v. p. 365; Xen. "Symp." ii. 7; Plut. "Lycurg." 19.

VI

There are other points in which this legislator's views run counter to those commonly accepted. Thus: in other states the individual citizen is master over his own children, domestics, (1) goods and chattels, and belongings generally; but Lycurgus, whose aim was to secure to all the citizens a considerable share in one another's goods without mutual injury, enacted that each one should have an equal power of his neighbour's children as over his own. (2) The principle is this. When a man knows that this, that, and the other person are fathers of children subject to his authority, he must perforce deal by them even as he desires his own child to be dealt by. And, if a boy chance to have received a whipping, not from his own father but some other, and goes and complains to his own father, it would be thought wrong on the part of that father if he did not inflict a second whipping on his son. A striking proof, in its way, how completely they trust each other not to impose dishonourable commands upon their children. (3)

(1) Or rather, "members of his household."

(2) See Plut. "Lycurg." 15 (Clough, i. 104).

(3) See Plut. "Moral." 237 D.

In the same way he empowered them to use their neighbour's (4) domestics in case of need. This communism he applied also to dogs used for the chase; in so far that a party in need of dogs will invite the owner to the chase, and if he is not at leisure to attend himself, at any rate he is happy to let his dogs go. The same applies to the use of horses. Some one has fallen sick perhaps, or is in want of a carriage, (5) or is anxious to reach some point or other quickly—in any case he has a right, if he sees a horse anywhere, to take and use it, and restores it safe and sound when he has done with it.

(4) See Aristot. "Pol." ii. 5 (Jowett, i. pp. xxxi. and 34; ii. p. 53); Plat. "Laws," viii. 845 A; Newman, "Pol. Aristot." ii. 249 foll.

(5) "Has not a carriage of his own."

And here is another institution attributed to Lycurgus which scarcely coincides with the customs elsewhere in vogue. A hunting party returns from the chase, belated. They want provisions—they have nothing prepared themselves. To meet this contingency he made it a rule that owners (6) are to leave behind the food that has been dressed; and the party in need will open the seals, take out what they want, seal up the remainder, and leave it. Accordingly, by his system of give-and-take even those with next to nothing (7) have a share in all that the country can supply, if ever they stand in need of anything.

(6) Reading {pepamenous}, or if {pepasmenous}, "who have already finished their repasts."

(7) See Aristot. "Pol." ii. 9 (Jowett, i. pp. xlii. and 52); Muller, "Dorians," iii. 10, 1 (vol. ii. 197, Eng. tr.)

VII

There are yet other customs in Sparta which Lycurgus instituted in opposition to those of the rest of Hellas, and the following among them. We all know that in the generality of states every one devotes his full energy to the business of making money: one man as a tiller of the soil, another as a mariner, a third as a merchant, whilst others depend on various arts to earn a living. But at Sparta Lycurgus forbade his freeborn citizens to have anything whatsoever to do with the concerns of money-making. As freemen, he enjoined upon them to regard as their concern exclusively those activities upon which the foundations of civic liberty are based.

And indeed, one may well ask, for what reason should wealth be regarded as a matter for serious pursuit (1) in a community where, partly by a system of equal contributions to the necessaries of life, and partly by the maintenance of a common standard of living, the lawgiver placed so effectual a check upon the desire of riches for the sake of luxury? What inducement, for instance, would there be to make money, even for the sake of wearing apparel, in a state where personal adornment is held to lie not in the costliness of the clothes they wear, but in the healthy condition of the body to be clothed? Nor again could there be much inducement to amass wealth, in order to be able to expend it on the members of a common mess, where the legislator had made it seem far more glorious that a man should help his fellows by the labour of his body than by costly outlay. The latter being, as he finely phrased it, the function of wealth, the former an activity of the soul.

(1) See Plut. "Lycurg." 10 (Clough, i. 96).

He went a step further, and set up a strong barrier (even in a society such as I have described) against the pursuance of money-making by wrongful means.

(2) In the first place, he established a coinage (3) of so extraordinary a sort, that even a single sum of ten minas (4) could not come into a house without attracting the notice, either of the master himself, or of some member of his household. In fact, it would occupy a considerable space, and need a waggon to carry it. Gold and silver themselves, moreover, are liable to search, (5) and in case of detection, the possessor subjected to a penalty. In fact, to repeat the question asked above, for what reason should money-making become an earnest pursuit in a community where the possession of wealth entails more pain than its employment brings satisfaction?

(2) Or, "against illegitimate commerce."

(3) See Plut. "Lycurg." 9 (Clough, i. 94).

(4) = 40 pounds, circa.

(5) See Grote, "H. G." ix. 320; Aristot. "Pol." ii. 9, 37.

VIII

But to proceed. We are all aware that there is no state (1) in the world in which greater obedience is shown to magistrates, and to the laws themselves, than Sparta. But, for my part, I am disposed to think that Lycurgus could never have attempted to establish this healthy condition, (2) until he had first secured the unanimity of the most powerful members of the state. I infer this for the following reasons. (3) In other states the leaders in rank and influence do not even desire to be thought to fear the magistrates. Such a thing they would regard as in itself a symbol of servility. In Sparta, on the contrary, the stronger a man is the more readily does he bow before constituted authority. And indeed, they magnify themselves on their humility, and on a prompt obedience, running, or at any rate not crawling with laggard step, at the word of command. Such an example of eager discipline, they are persuaded, set by themselves, will not fail to be followed by the rest. And this is precisely what has taken place. It (4) is reasonable to suppose that it was these same noblest members of the state who combined (5) to lay the foundation of the ephorate, after they had come to the conclusion themselves, that of all the blessings which a state, or an army, or a household, can enjoy, obedience is the greatest. Since, as they could not but reason, the greater the power with which men fence about authority, the greater the fascination it will exercise upon the mind of the citizen, to the enforcement of obedience.

(1) See Grote, "H. G." v. 516; "Mem." III. v. 18.

(2) Or, reading after L. Dindorf, {eutaxian}, "this world-renowned orderliness."

(3) Or, "from these facts."

(4) Or, "It was only natural that these same..."

(5) Or, "helped." See Aristot. "Pol." v. 11, 3; ii. 9, 1 (Jowett, ii.

224); Plut. "Lycurg." 7, 29; Herod. i. 65; Muller, "Dorians," iii. 7, 5 (vol. ii. p. 125, Eng. tr.)

Accordingly the ephors are competent to punish whomsoever they choose; they have power to exact fines on the spur of the moment; they have power to depose magistrates in mid career (6)—nay, actually to imprison them and bring them to trial on the capital charge. Entrusted with these vast powers, they do not, as do the rest of states, allow the magistrates elected to exercise authority as they like, right through the year of office; but, in the style rather of despotic monarchs, or presidents of the games, at the first symptom of an offence against the law they inflict chastisement without warning and without hesitation.

(6) Or, "before the expiration of their term of office." See Plut. "Agis," 18 (Clough, iv. 464); Cic. "de Leg." iii. 7; "de Rep." ii. 33.

But of all the many beautiful contrivances invented by Lycurgus to kindle a willing obedience to the laws in the hearts of the citizens, none, to my mind, was happier or more excellent than his unwillingness to deliver his code to the people at large, until, attended by the most powerful members of the state, he had betaken himself to Delphi, (7) and there made inquiry of the god whether it were better for Sparta, and conducive to her interests, to obey the laws which he had framed. And not until the divine answer came: "Better will it be in every way," did he deliver them, laying it down as a last ordinance that to refuse obedience to a code which had the sanction of the Pythian god himself (8) was a thing not illegal only, but profane.

(7) See Plut. "Lycurg." 5, 6, 29 (Clough, i. 89, 122); Polyb. x. 2, 9.

(8) Or, "a code delivered in Pytho, spoken by the god himself."

IX

The following too may well excite our admiration for Lycurgus. I speak of the consummate skill with which he induced the whole state of Sparta to regard an honourable death as preferable to an ignoble life. And indeed if any one will investigate the matter, he will find that by comparison with those who make it a principle to retreat in face of danger, actually fewer of these Spartans die in battle, since, to speak truth, salvation, it would seem, attends on virtue far more frequently than on cowardice—virtue, which is at once easier and sweeter, richer in resource and stronger of arm, (1) than her opposite. And that virtue has another familiar attendant—to wit, glory—needs no showing, since the whole world would fain ally themselves after some sort in battle with the good.

(1) See Homer, "Il." v. 532; Tyrtaeus, 11, 14, {tressanton d' andron pas' apolol arete}.

Yet the actual means by which he gave currency to these principles is a point which it were well not to overlook. It is clear that the lawgiver set himself deliberately to provide all the blessings of heaven for the good man, and a sorry and ill-starred existence for the coward.

In other states the man who shows himself base and cowardly wins to himself an evil reputation and the nickname of a coward, but that is all. For the rest he buys and sells in the same market-place as the good man; he sits beside him at play; he exercises with him in the same gymnasium, and all as suits his humour. But at Lacedaemon there is not one man who would notfeel ashamed to welcome the coward at the common mess-tabe, or to try conclusions with such an antagonist in a wrestling bout. Consider the day's round of his existence. The sides are being picked up in a football match, (2) but he is left out as the odd man: there is no place for him. During the choric dance (3) he is driven away into ignominious quarters. Nay, in the very streets it is he who must step aside for others to pass, or, being seated, he must rise and make room, even for a younger man. At home he will have his maiden relatives to support in isolation (and they will hold him to blame for their unwedded lives). (4) A hearth with no wife to bless it—that is a condition he must face, (5) and yet he will have to pay damages to the last farthing for incurring it. Let him not roam abroad with a smooth and smiling countenance;
(6) let him not imitate men whose fame is irreproachable, or he shall feel on his back the blows of his superiors. Such being the weight of infamy which is laid upon all cowards, I, for my part, am not surprised if in Sparta they deem death preferable to a life so steeped in dishonour and reproach.

(2) See Lucian, "Anacharsis," 38; Muller, "Dorians," (vol. ii. 309, Eng. tr.)

(3) The {khoroi}, e.g. of the Gymnopaedia. See Muller, op. cit. iv. 6, 4 (vol. ii. 334, Eng. tr.)

(4) {tes anandrias}, cf. Plut. "Ages." 30; or, {tes anandreias}, "they must bear the reproach of his cowardice."

(5) Omitting {ou}, or translate, "that is an evil not to be disregarded." See Dindorf, ad loc.; Sturz, "Lex. Xen." {Estia}.

(6) See Plut. "Ages." 30 (Clough, iv. 36); "Hell." VI. iv. 16.

X

That too was a happy enactment, in my opinion, by which Lycurgus provided for the continual cultivation of virtue, even to old age. By fixing (1) the election to the council of elders (2) as a last ordeal at the goal of life, he made it impossible for a high standard of virtuous living to be disregarded even in old age. (So, too, it is worthy of admiration in him that he lent his helping hand to virtuous old age. (3) Thus, by making the elders sole arbiters in the trial for life, he contrived to charge old age with a greater weight of honour than that which is accorded to the strength of mature manhood.) And assuredly such a contest as this must appeal to the zeal of mortal man beyond all others in a supreme degree. Fair, doubtless, are contests of gymnastic skill, yet are they but trials of bodily excellence, but this contest for the seniority is of a higher sort—it is an ordeal of the soul itself. In proportion, therefore, as the soul is worthier than the body, so must these contests of the soul appeal to a stronger enthusiasm than their bodily antitypes.

(1) Reading {protheis}. See Plut. "Lycurg." 26 (Clough. i. 118); Aristot. "Pol." ii. 9, 25.

(2) Or, "seniory," or "senate," or "board of elders"; lit. "the Gerontia."

(3) Or, "the old age of the good. Yet this he did when he made... since he contrived," etc.

And yet another point may well excite our admiration for Lycurgus largely. It had not escaped his observation that communities exist where those who are willing to make virtue their study and delight fail somehow in ability to add to the glory of their fatherland. (4) That lesson the legislator laid to heart, and in Sparta he enforced, as a matter of public duty, the practice of virtue by every citizen. And so it is that, just as man differs from man in some excellence, according as he cultivates or neglects to cultivate it, this city of Sparta, with good reason, outshines all other states in virtue; since she, and she alone, as made the attainment of a high standard of noble living a public duty.

(4) Is this an autobiographical touch?

And was this not a noble enactment, that whereas other states are content to inflict punishment only in cases where a man does wrong against his neighbour, Lycurgus imposed penalties no less severe on him who openly neglected to make himself as good as possible? For this, it seems, was his principle: in the one case, where a man is robbed, or defrauded, or kidnapped, and made a slave of, the injury of the misdeed, whatever it be, is personal to the individual so maltreated; but in the other case whole communities suffer foul treason at the hands of the base man and the coward. So that it was only reasonable, in my opinion, that he should visit the heaviest penalty upon these latter.

Moreover, he laid upon them, like some irresistible necessity, the obligation to cultivate the whole virtue of a citizen. Provided they duly performed the injunctions of the law, the city belonged to them, each and all, in absolute possession and on an equal footing. Weakness of limb or want of wealth (5) was no drawback in his eyes. But as for him who, out of the cowardice of his heart, shrank from the painful performance of the law's injunction, the finger of the legislator pointed him out as there and then disqualified to be regarded longer as a member of the brotherhood of peers. (6)

(5) But see Aristot. "Pol." ii. 9, 32.

(6) Grote, "H. G." viii. 81; "Hell." III. iii. 5.

It may be added, that there was no doubt as to the great antiquity of this code of laws. The point is clear so far, that Lycurgus himself is said to have lived in the days of the Heraclidae. (7) But being of so long standing, these laws, even at this day, still are stamped in the eyes of other men with all the novelty of youth. And the most marvellous thing of all is that, while everybody is agreed to praise these remarkable institutions, there is not a single state which cares to imitate them.

(7) See Plut. "Lycurg." 1.

XI

The above form a common stock of blessings, open to every Spartan to enjoy, alike in peace and in war. But if any one desires to be informed in what way the legislator improved upon the ordinary machinery of warfare and in reference to an army in the field, it is easy to satisfy his curiosity.

In the first instance, the ephors announce by proclamation the limit of age to which the service applies (1) for cavalry and heavy infantry; and in the next place, for the various handicraftsmen. So that, even on active service, the Lacedaemonians are well supplied with all the conveniences enjoyed by people living as citizens at home. (2) All implements and instruments whatsoever, which an army may need in common, are ordered to be in readiness, (3) some on waggons and others on baggage animals. In this way anything omitted can hardly escape detection.

(1) I.e. "in the particular case." See "Hell." VI. iv. 17; Muller, "Dorians," iii. 12 (vol. ii. 242 foll., Eng. tr.)

(2) Or, "the conveniences of civil life at home."

(3) Reading {parekhein}, or if {paragein}, "to be conveyed." Cf. Pausan. I. xix. 1. See "Cyrop." VI. ii. 34.

For the actual encounter under arms, the following inventions are attributed to him. The soldier has a crimson-coloured uniform and a heavy shield of bronze; his theory being that such an equipment has no sort of feminine association, and is altogether most warrior-like. (4) It is most quickly burnished; it is least readily soiled. (5)

(4) Cf. Aristoph. "Acharn." 320, and the note of the scholiast.

(5) See Ps. Plut. "Moral." 238 F.

He further permitted those who were above the age of early manhood to wear their hair long. (6) For so, he conceived, they would appear of larger stature, more free and indomitable, and of a more terrible aspect.

(6) See Plut. "Lycurg." 22 (Clough, i. 114).

So furnished and accoutred, he divided his citizen soldiers into six morai (7) (or regimental divisions) of cavalry (8) and heavy infantry. Each of these citizen regiments (political divisions) has one polemarch (9) (or colonel), four lochagoi (or captains of companies), eight penteconters (or lieutenants, each in command of half a company), and sixteen enomotarchs (or commanders of sections). At the word of command any such regimental division can be formed readily either into enomoties (i.e. single file) or into threes (i.e. three files abreast), or into sixes (i.e. six files abreast). (10)

(7) The {mora}. Jowett, "Thuc." ii. 320, note to Thuc. v. 68, 3.

(8) See Plut. "Lycurg." 23 (Clough, i. 115); "Hell." VI. iv. 11; Thuc. v. 67; Paus. IV. viii. 12.

(9) See Thuc. v. 66, 71.

(10) See Thuch. v. 68, and Arnold's note ad loc.; "Hell." VI. iv. 12; "Anab." II. iv. 26; Rustow and Kochly, op. cit. p. 117.

As to the idea, commonly entertained, that the tactical arrangement of the Laconian heavy infantry is highly complicated, no conception could be more opposed to fact. For in the Laconian order the front rank men are all leaders, (11) so that each file has everything necessary to play its part efficiently. In fact, this disposition is so easy to understand that no one who can distinguish one human being from another could fail to follow it. One set have the privilege of leaders, the other the duty of followers. The evolutional orders, (12) by which greater depth or shallowness is given to the battle line, are given by word of mouth by the enomotarch (or commander of the section), who plays the part of the herald, and they cannot be mistaken. None of these manouvres presents any difficulty whatsoever to the understanding.

(11) See "Anab." IV. iii. 26; "Cyrop." III. iii. 59; VI. iii. 22.

(12) I.e. "for doubling depth"; e.g. anglice, "form two deep," etc., when marching to a flank. Grote, "H. G." vii. 108; Thuc. v. 66; also Rustow and Kochly, op. cit. p. 111, S. 8, note 19; p. 121, $17, note 41.

But when it comes to their ability to do battle equally well in spite of some confusion which has been set up, and whatever the chapter of accidents may confront them with, (13) I admit that the tactics here are not so easy to understand, except for people trained under the laws of Lycurgus. Even movements which an instructor in heavy-armed warfare (14) might look upon as difficult are performed by the Lacedaemonians with the utmost ease. (15) Thus, the troops, we will suppose, are marching in column; one section of a company is of course stepping up behind another from the rear. (16) Now, if at such a moment a hostile force appears in front in battle order, the word is passed down to the commander of each section, "Deploy (into line) to the left." And so throughout the whole length of the column, until the line is formed facing the enemy. Or supposing while in this position an enemy appears in the rear. Each file performs a counter-march (17) with the effect of bringing the best men face to face with the enemy all along the line. (18) As to the point that the leader previously on the right finds himself now on the left, (19) they do not consider that they are necessarily losers thereby, but, as it may turn out, even gainers. If, for instance, the enemy attempted to turn their flank, he would find himself wrapping round, not their exposed, but their shielded flank. (20) Or if, for any reason, it be thought advisable for the general to keep the right wing, they turn the corps about, (21) and counter- march by ranks, until the leader is on the right, and the rear rank on the left. Or again, supposing a division of the enemy appears on the right whilst they are marching in column, they have nothing further to do but to wheel each company to the right, like a trireme, prow forwards, (22) to meet the enemy, and thus the rear company again finds itself on the right. If, however, the enemy should attack on the left, either they will not allow of that and push him aside, (23) or else they wheel their companies to the left to face the antagonist, and thus the rear company once more falls into position on the left.

(13) Or, "alongside of any comrade who may have fallen in their way." See Plut. "Pelop." 23 (Clough, ii. 222); Thuc. v. 72.

(14) Or, "drill sergeant."

(15) See Jebb, note to "Theophr." viii. 3.

(16) Or, "marching in rear of another."

(17) See Rustow and Kochly, p. 127.

(18) Or, "every time."

(19) See Thuc. v. 67, 71.

(20) See Rustow and Kochly, p. 127.

(21) For these movements, see "Dict. of Antiq." "Exercitus"; Grote, "H. G." vii. 111.

(22) See "Hell." VII. v. 23.

(23) I am indebted to Professor Jebb for the following suggestions with regard to this passage: "The words {oude touto eosin, all apothousin e}, etc., contain some corruption. The sense ought clearly to be roughly parallel with that of the phrase used a little before, {ouden allo pragmateuontai e}, etc. Perhaps {apothousin} is a corruption of {apothen ousin}, and this corruption occasioned the insertion of {e}. Probably Xenophon wrote {oude touto eosin, all apothen ousin antipalous}, etc.: 'while the enemy is still some way off, they turn their companies so as to face him.' The words {apothen ousin} indirectly suggest the celerity of the Spartan movement."

XII

I will now speak of the mode of encampment sanctioned by the regulation of Lycurgus. To avoid the waste incidental to the angles of a square, (1) the encampment, according to him, should be circular, except where there was the security of a hill, (2) or fortification, or where they had a river in their rear. He had sentinels posted during the day along the place of arms and facing inwards; (3) since they are appointed not so much for the sake of the enemy as to keep an eye on friends. The enemy is sufficiently watched by mounted troopers perched on various points commanding the widest prospect.

(1) Or, "Regarding the angles of a square as a useless inconvenience, he arranged that an encampment should be circular," etc. See Polyb. vi. 31, 42.

(2) Cf. "Hell." VI. iv. 14; Polyaen. II. iii. 11, ap. Schneider.

(3) Lit. "these," {tas men}. Or, "He had lines of sentinels posted throughout the day; one line facing inwards towards the place of arms (and these were appointed, etc.); while observation of the enemy was secured by mounted troopers," etc.

To guard against hostile approach by night, sentinel duty according to the ordinance was performed by the Sciritae (4) outside the main body. At the present time the rule is so far modified that the duty is entrusted to foreigners, (5) if there be a foreign contingent present, with a leaven of Spartans themselves to keep them company. (6)

(4) See Muller's "Dorians," ii. 253; "Hell." VI. v. 24; "Cyrop." IV. ii. 1; Thuc. v. 67, 71; Grote, "H. G." vii. 110.

(5) See "Hipparch." ix. 4.

(6) Reading {auton de}. The passage is probably corrupt. See L. Dindorf ad loc.

The custom of always taking their spears (7) with them when they go their rounds must certainly be attributed to the same cause which makes them exclude their slaves from the place of arms. Nor need we be surprised if, when retiring for necessary purposes, they only withdraw just far enough from one another, or from the place of arms itself, not to create annoyance. The need of precaution is the whole explanation.

(7) See Critias, ap. Schneider ad loc.

The frequency with which they change their encampments is another point. It is done quite as much for the sake of benefiting their friends as of annoying their enemies.

Further, the law enjoins upon all Lacedaemonians, during the whole period of an expedition, the constant practice of gymnastic (8) exercises, whereby their pride (9) in themselves is increased, and they appear freer and of a more liberal aspect than the rest of the world. (10) The walk and the running ground must not exceed in length (11) the space covered by a regimental division, (12) so that no one may find himself far from his own stand of arms. After the gymnastic exercises the senior polemarch gives the order (by herald) to be seated. This serves all the purposes of an inspection. After this the order is given "to get breakfast," and for "the outposts (13) to be relieved." After this, again, come pastimes and relaxations before the evening exercises, after which the herald's cry is heard "to take the evening meal." When they have sung a hymn to the gods to whom the offerings of happy omen had been performed, the final order, "Retire to rest at the place of arms," (14) is given.

(8) Cf. Herod. vii. 208; Plut. "Lycurg." 22 (Clough, i. 113 foll.)

(9) Reading {megalophronesterous} (L. Dindorf's emendation) for the vulg. {megaloprepesterous}. Xen "Opusc. polit." Ox. MDCCCLVI.

(10) Or, "the proud self-consciousness of their own splendour is increased, and by comparison with others they bear more notably the impress of freemen."

(11) The word {masso} is "poetical" (old Attic?). See "Cyrop." II. iv. 27, and L. Dindorf ad loc.

(12) A single mora, or an army corps.

(13) Or, "vedettes," {proskopon}. See "Cyrop." V. ii. 6.

(14)? Or, "on your arms." See Sturz, "Lex. Xen." s.v.

If the story is a little long the reader must not be surprised, since it would be difficult to find any point in military matters omitted by the Lacedaemonians which seems to demand attention.

XIII

I will now give a detailed account of the power and privilege assigned by Lycurgus to the king during a campaign. To begin with, so long as he is on active service, the state maintains the king and those with him. (1) The polemarchs mess with him and share his quarters, so that by dint of constant intercourse they may be all the better able to consult in common in case of need. Besides the polemarch three other members of the peers (2) share the royal quarters, mess, etc. The duty of these is to attend to all matters of commisariat, (3) in order that the king and the rest may have unbroken leisure to attend to affairs of actual warfare.

(1) I.e. "the Thirty." See "Ages." i. 7; "Hell." III. iv. 2; Plut. "Ages." 6 (Clough, iv. 6); Aristot. "Pol." ii. 9, 29.

(2) For these {oi omoioi}, see "Cyrop." I. v. 5; "Hell." III. iii. 5.

(3) Lit. "supplies and necessaries."

But I will resume at a somewhat higher point and describe the manner in which the king sets out on an expedition. As a preliminary step, before leaving home he offers sacrifice (in company with (4) his staff) to Zeus

Agetor (the Leader), and if the victims prove favourable then and there the priest, (5) who bears the sacred fire, takes thereof from off the altar and leads the way to the boundaries of the land. Here for the second time the king does sacrifice (6) to Zeus and Athena; and as soon as the offerings are accepted by those two divinities he steps across the boundaries of the land. And all the while the fire from those sacrifices leads the way, and is never suffered to go out. Behind follow beasts for sacrifice of every sort.

(4) Lit. reading {kai oi sun auto}, after L. Dindorf, "he and those with him."

(5) Lit. "the Purphuros." See Nic. Damasc. ap. Stob. "Fl." 44, 41; Hesych. ap. Schneider, n. ad loc.

(6) These are the {diabateria}, so often mentioned in the "Hellenica."

Invariably when he offers sacrifice the king begins the work in the gloaming ere the day has broken, being minded to anticipate the goodwill of the god. And round about the place of sacrifice are present the polemarchs and captains, the lieutenants and sub-lieutenants, with the commandants of the baggage train, and any general of the states (7) who may care to assist. There, too, are to be seen two of the ephors, who neither meddle nor make, save only at the summons of the king, yet have they their eyes fixed on the proceedings of each one there and keep all in order, (8) as may well be guessed. When the sacrifices are accomplished the king summons all and issues his orders (9) as to what has to be done. And all with such method that, to witness the proceedings, you might fairly suppose the rest of the world to be but bungling experimenters, (10) and the Lacedaemonians alone true handicraftsmen in the art of soldiering.

(7) I.e. "allied"? or "perioecid"?

(8) {sophronizousin}, "keep every one in his sober senses."

(9) See Thuc. v. 66.

(10) {autoskhediastai, tekhnitai}. See Jebb, "Theophr." x. 3.

Anon the king puts himself at the head of the troops, and if no enemy appears he heads the line of march, no one preceding him except the Sciritae, and the mounted troopers exploring in front. (11) If, however, there is any reason to anticipate a battle, the king takes the leading column of the first army corps (12) and wheels to the right until he has got into position with two army corps and two generals of division on either flank. The disposition of the supports is assigned to the eldest of the royal council (13) (or staff corps) acting as brigadier—the staff consisting of all peers who share the royal mess and quarters, with the soothsayers, surgeons, (14) and pipers, whose place is in the front of the troops, (15) with, finally, any volunteers who happen to be present. So that there is no check or hesitation in anything to be done; every contingency is provided for.

(11) Or, "who are on scouting duty. If, however, they expect a battle," etc.

(12) Technically, "mora."

(13) {ton peri damosian}. See "Hell." IV. v. 8; vii. 4.

(14) See "Anab." III. iv. 30; "Cyrop." I. vi. 15; L. Dindorf, n. ad loc.

(15) Schneider refers to Polyaenus, i. 10.

The following details also seem to me of high utility among the inventions of Lycurgus with a view to the final arbitrament of battle. Whensoever, the enemy being now close enough to watch the proceedings, (16) the goat is sacrificed; then, says the law, let all the pipers, in their places, play upon the pipes, and let every Lacedaemonian don a wreath. Then, too, so runs the order, let the shields be brightly polished. The privilege is accorded to the young man to enter battle with his long locks combed. (17) To be of cheery countenance—that, too, is of good repute. Onwards they pass the word of command to the subaltern (18) in command of his section, since it is impossible to hear along the whole of each section from the particular subaltern posted on the outside. It devolves, finally, on the polemarch to see that all goes well.

(16) See Plut. "Lycurg." 22 (Clough, i. 114); and for the goat sacrificed to Artemis Agrotera, see "Hell." IV. ii. 20; Pause. IX. xiii. 4; Plut. "Marcell." 22 (Clough, ii. 264).

(17) See Plut. "Lycurg." 22 (Clough, i. 114). The passage is corrupt, and possibly out of its place. I cite the words as they run in the MSS. with various proposed emendations. See Schneider, n. ad loc. {exesti de to neo kai kekrimeno eis makhen sunienai kai phaidron einai kai eudokimon. kai parakeleuontai de k.t.l.} Zeune, {kekrimeno komen}, after Plut. "Lycurg." 22. Weiske, {kai komen diakekrimeno}. Cobet, {exesti de to neo liparo kai tas komas diakekrimeno eis makhen ienai}.

(18) Lit. "to the enomotarch."

When the right moment for encamping has come, the king is responsible for that, and has to point out the proper place. The despatch of emissaries, however, whether to friends or to foes, is (not) (19) the king's affair. Petitioners in general wishing to transact anything treat, in the first instance, with the king. If the case concerns some point of justice, the king despatches the petitioner to the Hellanodikai (who form the court-martial); if of money, to the paymasters. (20) If the petitioner brings booty, he is sent off to the Laphuropolai (or sellers of spoil). This being the mode of procedure, no other duty is left to the king, whilst he is on active service, except to play the part of priest in matters concerning the gods and of commander-in-chief in his relationship to men. (21)

(19) The MSS. give {au}, "is again," but the word {mentoi}, "however,"

and certain passages in "Hell." II. ii. 12, 13; II. iv. 38 suggest the negative {ou} in place of {au}. If {au} be right, then we should read {ephoren} in place of {basileos}, "belongs to the ephors."

(20) Technically the {tamiai}.

(21) See Aristot. "Pol." iii. 14.

XIV (1)

Now, if the question be put to me, Do you maintain that the laws of Lycurgus remain still to this day unchanged? that indeed is an assertion which I should no longer venture to maintain; knowing, as I do, that in former times the Lacedaemonians preferred to live at home on moderate means, content to associate exclusively with themselves rather than to play the part of governor-general (2) in foreign states and to be corrupted by flattery; knowing further, as I do, that formerly they dreaded to be detected in the possession of gold, whereas nowadays there are not a few who make it their glory and their boast to be possessed of it. I am very well aware that in former days alien acts (3) were put in force for this very object. To live abroad was not allowed. And why? Simply in order that the citizens of Sparta might not take the infection of dishonesty and light-living from foreigners; whereas now I am very well aware that those who are reputed to be leading citizens have but one ambition, and that is to live to the end of their days as governors-general on a foreign soil. (4) The days were when their sole anxiety was to fit themselves to lead the rest of Hellas. But nowadays they concern themselves much more to wield command than to be fit themselves to rule. And so it has come to pass that whereas in old days the states of Hellas flocked to Lacedaemon seeking her leadership (5) against the supposed wrongdoer, now numbers are inviting one another to prevent the Lacedaemonians again recovering their empire. (6) Yet, if they have incurred all these reproaches, we need not wonder, seeing that they are so plainly disobedient to the god himself and to the laws of their own lawgiver Lycurgus.

(1) For the relation of this chapter to the rest of the treatise, see Grote, ix. 325; Ern. Naumann, "de Xen. libro qui" {LAK. POLITEIA} inscribitur, p. 18 foll.; Newmann, "Pol. Aristot." ii. 326.

(2) Harmosts.

(3) "Xenelasies," {xenelasiai} technically called. See Plut. "Lycurg." 27; "Agis," 10; Thuc. ii. 39, where Pericles contrasts the liberal spirit of the democracy with Spartan exclusiveness; "Our city is thrown open to the world, and we never expel a foreigner or prevent him from seeing or learning anything of which the secret, if revealed to an enemy, might profit him."—Jowett, i. 118.

(4) Lit. "harmosts"; and for the taste of living abroad, see what is said of Dercylidas, "Hell." IV. iii. 2. The harmosts were not removed till just before Leuctra (371 B.C.), "Hell." VI. iv. 1, and after, see Paus. VIII. lii. 4; IX. lxiv.

(5) See Plut. "Lycurg." 30 (Clough, i. 124).

(6) This passage would seem to fix the date of the chapter xiv. as about the time of the Athenian confederacy of 378 B.C.; "Hell." V. iv. 34; "Rev." v. 6. See also Isocr. "Panegyr." 380 B.C.; Grote, "H. G." ix. 325. See the text of a treaty between Athens, Chios, Mytilene, and Byzantium; Kohler, "Herm." v. 10; Rangabe, "Antiq. Hellen." ii. 40, 373; Naumann, op. cit. 26.

XV

I wish to explain with sufficient detail the nature of the covenant between king and state as instituted by Lycurgus; for this, I take it, is the sole type of rule (1) which still preserves the original form in which it was first established; whereas other constitutions will be found either to have been already modified or else to be still undergoing modifications at this moment.

(1) Or, "magistracy"; the word {arkhe} at once signifies rule and governmental office.

Lycurgus laid it down as law that the king shall offer in behalf of the state all public sacrifices, as being himself of divine descent, (2) and whithersoever the state shall despatch her armies the king shall take the lead. He granted him to receive honorary gifts of the things offered in sacrifice, and he appointed him choice land in many of the provincial cities, enough to satisfy moderate needs without excess of wealth. And in order that the kings also might camp and mess in public he appointed them public quarters; and he honoured them with a double portion (3) each at the evening meal, not in order that they might actually eat twice as much as others, but that the king might have wherewithal to honour whomsoever he desired. He also granted as a gift to each of the two kings to choose two mess-fellows, which same are called Puthioi. He also granted them to receive out of every litter of swine one pig, so that the king might never be at a loss for victims if in aught he wished to consult the gods.

(2) I.e. a Heracleid, in whichever line descended, and, through Heracles, from Zeus himself. The kings are therefore "heroes," i.e. demigods. See below; and for their privileges, see Herod. vi. 56, 57.

(3) See "Ages." v. 1.

Close by the palace a lake affords an unrestricted supply of water; and how useful that is for various purposes they best can tell who lack the luxury. (4) Moreover, all rise from their seats to give place to the king, save only that the ephors rise not from their thrones of office. Monthly they exchange oaths, the ephors in behalf of the state, the king himself in his own behalf. And this is the oath on the king's part: "I will exercise my kingship in accordance with the established laws of the state." And on the part of the state the oath runs: "So long as he (5) (who exercises kingship) shall abide by his oaths we will not suffer his kingdom to be shaken." (6)

(4) See Hartman, "An. Xen. N." p. 274; but cf. "Cyneget." v. 34;

"Anab." V. iii. 8.

(5) Lit. "he yonder."

(6) Lit. "we will keep it for him unshaken." See L. Dindorf, n. ad loc. and praef. p. 14 D.

These then are the honours bestowed upon the king during his lifetime (at home) (7)—honours by no means much exceeding those of private citizens, since the lawgiver was minded neither to suggest to the kings the pride of the despotic monarch, (8) nor, on the other hand, to engender in the heart of the citizen envy of their power. As to those other honours which are given to the king at his death, (9) the laws of Lycurgus would seem plainly to signify hereby that these kings of Lacedaemon are not mere mortals but heroic beings, and that is why they are preferred in honour. (10)

(7) The words "at home" look like an insertion.

(8) Lit. "the tyrant's pride."

(9) See "Hell." III. iii. 1; "Ages." xi. 16; Herod. vi. 58.

(10) Intentionally or not on the part of the writer, the concluding words, in which the intention of the Laws is conveyed, assume a metrical form:

{oukh os anthropous all os eroas tous
Lakedaimonion basileis protetimekasin.}

See Ern. Naumann, op. cit. p. 18.

www.ingramcontent.com/pod-product-compliance
Lightning Source LLC
Chambersburg PA
CBHW060800310726
48980CB00002B/170

* 9 7 8 3 7 3 2 6 2 0 9 1 3 *